Disney
FROZEN

Written by Veronica Wagner
Illustrated by Art Mawhinney and the Disney Storybook Art Team

we make books come alive®
pi kids Phoenix International Publications, Inc.
Chicago • London • New York • Hamburg • Mexico City • Sydney

When Olaf first met Anna and Kristoff, he knew very little about the world. But he was eager to join in and couldn't wait to find friendship, sunshine, and warm hugs.

Summer is coming to Arendelle… but it hasn't arrived quite yet. In the meantime, can you spot these chilly crystals?

It might seem a little strange for a snowman to like sunny weather, but Elsa gave Olaf his own personal snow flurry, and now he's *always* cool!

Who else is enjoying the sunshine at the beach? Take a look and find these summery sidekicks:

whale

seal

this crab

this fish

this seagull

sea star

When it's time for a party in Arendelle, everyone pitches in to help. And nothing's cozier than a nice warm snowman…cookie.

Cookies are here, there, and everywhere! Can you spot these toothsome tidbits?

Everybody wants to win the bubble-blowing contest. And Olaf ends up inside one of the bubbles!

Bubbles aren't the only things afloat in Arendelle. Can you find these airborne articles?

kite

this bird

this butterfly

balloon

dragonfly

cloud

Olaf is posing for a new portrait—painted by Anna! Soon his picture will be on display in Arendelle's Gallery of Friends.

Olaf's portrait will join these centerpieces of the palace art collection. Can you find them all?

Kristoff's portrait

painted heart

statue of Anna

troll jewels

bust of Sven

Elsa's portrait

Today Arendelle is celebrating Winter in Summer Day, with treats just as chilly as Olaf.

There are lots of frozen treats to feast on here. Do you see all of these delicious desserts?

this ice pop

chocolate bombe

banana split

parfait

ice cream sandwich

this ice cream cone

Arendelle is beautiful in winter white, but Olaf thinks it's even prettier in summertime colors. The ship is sailing across the fjord—and Olaf gets to steer!

It's a rainbow-bright day on the fjord! Can you spot these colorful waterside residents?

yellow duckling

orange fish

red fox

this green frog

violet newt

this blue kingfisher

At the end of one special day with his friends, Olaf is looking forward to… another special day with his friends. He can't wait to see everyone again tomorrow!

Twinkle, twinkle, little fireflies! See if you can find these six tiny sparklers:

Olaf and his friends aren't alone on North Mountain. Move back to the mountainside and find these animal onlookers:

bear cub

ermine

hawk

deer

fox

this squirrel

Swim back to the sandy beach and see if you can dig up these castle-building tools:

flag

this seashell

watering can

Olaf's snow flurry

shovel

bucket

It takes a lot of food to feed all of Arendelle! Charge back to the kitchen and find this batch of kitchen fixings:

this icing bag

butter crock

FLOUR

sugar canister

SUGAR

BUTTER

bag of flour

walnuts

mixing bowl

Olaf was caught in a bubble—and so were a few other things. Float back to the contest and find these bubbles before they pop!

flower

troll tot

snowflake

jewel

butterfly

bee

To make a statue, Elsa needs only her magic. But other artists need art supplies. Go back to the gallery and look for these artistic aids:

ruler

glue

palette

sketchbook

brush jar

this paint tube

Everyone loves fruit-flavored treats! Stroll back to the festival and find these ice cream add-ons:

cherries

bananas

oranges

pineapple

strawberries

blueberries

To keep the friends on course to Troll Valley, ramble back to the river and check off these way-finding widgets:

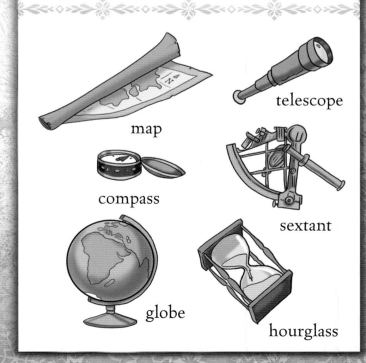

map

telescope

compass

sextant

globe

hourglass

What's shining along with the Northern Lights? Step back to the nighttime show and search for these glowing goods:

lantern

candle

campfire

lamp

luminaria

this torch